Presented to

With love from

Date

For my favorite people in the whole world . . .
Kaylie, Cassidy, Caleb, Cole and Claire.
-RW

To my mother and father, for their infinite kindness.
-CS

ZONDERKIDZ

God's Great Love for You

Requests for information should be addressed to:

Zonderkidz, *3900 Sparks Drive SE, Grand Rapids, Michigan 49546*

ISBN 978-0-310-75247-9

Design: Ron Huizinga

Printed in China

17 18 19 20 21 /DSC/ 20 19 18 17 16 15 14 13 12 11 10 9 8 7 6 5 4 3 2 1

God's Great Love for You

God's great love . . .

created the entire universe

And everything in it

Including you.

And he loves you with a great big unstoppable love.

Deeper than all the oceans

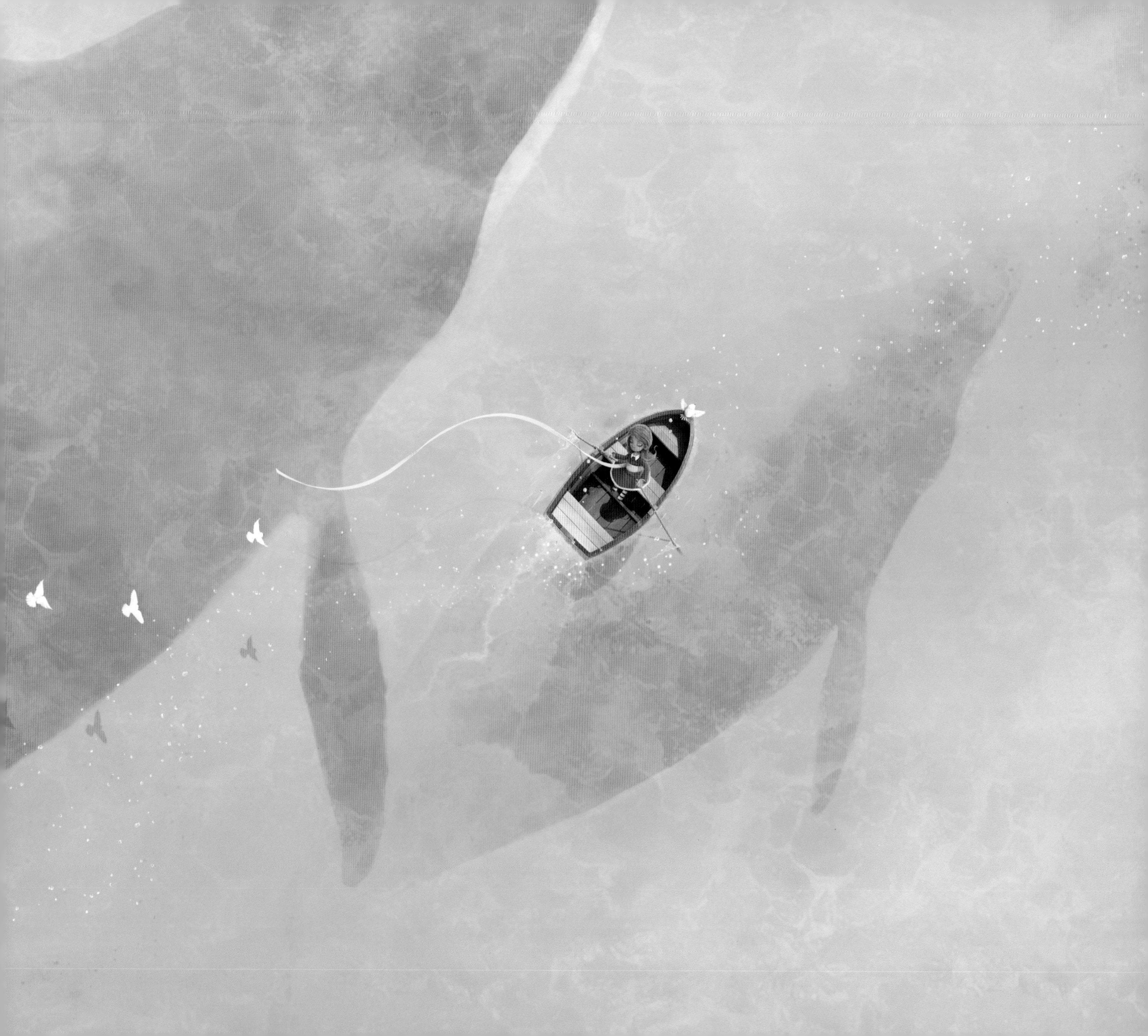

Higher than the moon and the stars

Wider than the big blue sky.

God's great love for you is with you wherever you go

On good days

And bad days

When you go to sleep at night

And when you wake up in the morning.

God's great love for you is . . .

perfect.

And everywhere

And will never end.